W9-BYC-286

RANDY ROBIN
FINDS A FRIEND

by Vilma Zuliani

illustrated by
Robert de Claire

hermitage press

130 Shepard Street   Lawrence, Mass. 01843

COPYRIGHT © 1977 BY VILMA ZULIANI
ALL RIGHTS RESERVED INCLUDING THE RIGHT
TO REPRODUCE THIS BOOK OR PARTS THEREOF IN ANY FORM
LIBRARY OF CONGRESS CATALOG CARD NUMBER: 77-74629
ISBN: 0-89441-002-4
PRINTED IN THE U. S. A.
GRAPHIC   LITHO

RANDY ROBIN FINDS A FRIEND

Once upon a time, not very long ago, a little robin lived in the top of a tall tree at the edge of a woods. His home was a nest which his mother and father had built early last spring.

They worked very hard to make the nest sturdy using twigs and grass and other things which they found lying around. On the inside, they covered it with down feathers to make it soft.

No sooner had they finished building their new home when the mother robin laid five beautiful pale blue eggs. Then both parents took turns sitting on the eggs to make certain they were kept nice and warm.

Early one morning in May the five little robins were born. They cracked their shells and wriggled out shaking their heads and crawling all over each other. Oh, you should have seen how funny they were. They had no feathers and they looked bald and naked. Their eyes were shut but they had big mouths with yellow lips which they opened wide, hoping to get something to eat.

And how they could eat! You have never seen anything like it. They would climb all over each other, stretching their necks and chirping for worms. (Little robins, you know, like worms about as much as little children like candy).

The poor mother and father robin were exhausted trying to feed them. The bigger they grew, the more they ate until neither the mother or father bird had a chance to swallow one worm for themselves. They just flew back and forth all day long bringing worms to their babies, who never seemed to get enough.

Finally, the parents decided that it was time to teach the little birds how to fly and to find food for themselves. By this time the five little robins had fluffy feathers and they weren't quite so awkward anymore.

At first, however, they had a hard time. Although they wanted to fly very much, they were afraid to try. The mother and father robin had to coax them, and finally, they even had to push them out of the nest.

This was true of all the robins except Randy, the littlest one. He was much bolder than the rest, and he was determined to fly first. It was still several days before the mother robin thought they were ready. When she saw him stand up in the nest and shake his wings, she warned him to quiet down and wait. Oh, it was hard for Randy because he was restless and much more adventurous than his brothers and sisters. All day long Randy would beg his mother and father to let him fly. Finally, one day, they agreed.

Randy stood up in the nest and pushed his brothers and sisters out of the way. His parents were on a nearby branch watching him and telling him what to do. Unlike the other little robins, Randy didn't need much coaxing and he didn't like to be taught. He felt big and strong and he was certain that he could make it on his own.

He stepped onto the rim of the nest and looked over the side. It was a long way to the ground, but that didn't stop him. He just took a deep breath and jumped, flapping his wings and chirping as loud as he could. However, no matter how hard he flapped, he just went down, down, down until he landed with a bump on the ground.

His parents quickly flew to the ground to see if he was hurt. He certainly didn't feel too good, I can tell you. The ground wasn't as soft as the nest, and Randy learned that fast enough. But even this didn't stop him. He didn't even cry. He just shook himself off a little, and looked at his wings, and cleaned off his dusty feathers, and then decided to try again.

Trying to get off the ground was even harder than getting there in the first place. Nevertheless, Randy wouldn't give up. No, not that bold little robin! With his mother and father coaching him and lifting him with their wings, he finally made it. What a great day that was for him! You can't imagine how proud he was, and how he bragged to his brothers and sisters who looked on at all this from their cozy little nest. It made them more afraid to fly than ever.

In teaching the others, the mother and father robin would point to Randy and say, "If he can do it, why can't you? You're so much bigger than he is." But every time any of them climbed onto the edge of the nest and looked down, they grew frightened and said: "We don't feel ready yet, maybe we should wait until tomorrow."

This made Randy laugh and he teased them until his two little sisters cried.

Actually, it was four days before they finally got out of the nest. And they did so only because the father robin lost patience with them and told them that if they didn't

get out on their own he would push them out. Well, the last two little robins had to be pushed, but finally, all of them learned to fly.

Once they did, they all loved it. What a great feeling to be able to fly in the air looking down on the woods, and further on, at the little houses in the town nearby. Next, the mother and father robin had to teach them how to look for food. The little robins were taught what to eat and where to find it. Little robins eat seeds and crumbs and insects and many other things but their favorite food, by far, is worms. You should have seen the five little robins look for worms and pull them out of the ground. The worms seemed to be bigger than they were, and yet they would gobble them in an instant.

Randy was the only little robin who wanted to go farther and farther away. He wasn't as interested in food as he was in flying. One night the mother robin looked at him and said, "How thin you are. Don't you eat?" Randy answered, "I'd rather explore than look for food, but whenever I <u>am</u> hungry, I can always find a worm."

"Where did you go today?" asked his father.

"Today I went into town and dug for worms in the gardens behind the houses," said Randy.

"That is a good place, I agree, but you had better be careful of the cats."

"Oh," said Randy boldly, "I saw two or three cats today, but they didn't frighten me. Cats can't fly and I can."

His little brothers and sisters shivered just to hear the word "cat." They remembered the day their parents had taken them to see what a cat looked like. They had gone into town, and the father robin flew low over a big orange cat who was sitting on the back porch of one of the houses. Just the look that cat gave them made them so frightened, they screamed and chirped and begged their mother and father to come away and fly back with them. Almost every one of them had nightmares that night. Except, of course, the littlest robin, Randy, who said that that old cat didn't frighten him! Not one bit.

"All the same," said mother robin, "although a cat can't fly, you'll think he can, he's so fast. And if you're busy pulling up a worm, and he comes up behind you, you won't have a chance to fly away." But Randy just shook his head and said that he wasn't afraid of any old cat.

Another thing that mother and father robin warned their littlest robin about, was flying too far from home. "Where were you all day today?" asked father robin. "Your mother and I were looking all over for you. You're too young to be flying off all alone. We've told you over and over to stay around home."

"I wasn't too far," answered Randy.

"Well, just where were you?" asked his mother.

"I was in that beautiful big tree with the purple leaves," answered Randy. "That's my favorite tree. It's so big, it's the biggest tree in all the woods."

"Oh I agree," said the mother bird, "it certainly is. It's called a purple beech. And wait until you see it this fall. All the leaves turn a deep purple; it's magnificent. When the sun sets, the entire tree appears radiant. But I agree with your father that you go too far from home. One of these days you're going to get lost."

"Oh, not me," said the littlest robin, "not me, I can always find my way home. No matter where I go, I never get lost because all I have to do is fly very high over the woods and spot that purple beech, and then I know my way from there."

"You're a little over confident," said the father robin, "and that always leads to trouble."

The next morning Randy got up at the crack of dawn and flew off before anyone else was up. That day he felt stronger and bolder than ever. He decided to go beyond the woods and beyond the town to where he had never been before. In fact, he liked to be able to come home and tell his brothers and sisters, in front of his parents, about all the new and exciting experiences he had. He especially liked to tell them about places that even his mother or father hadn't seen.

On this day the weather was perfect. Not a cloud was in the sky. It was barely daybreak when Randy flew into the back yard of a little white house, and started looking for a breakfast of worms. How good and juicy they were. And so many of them!

All of a sudden he saw the bush in front of him move. This puzzled him and he stood still, watching it. Then, as quick as lightening, the big orange cat sprang out at him. Poor Randy didn't have a chance to move. He was stunned.

It was a very lucky thing that a branch of the bush snapped back, just as the cat sprang, setting him off balance, or that would have been the end of our poor little bird. As it was, he barely flew out of the way before the cat made another leap at him with his claws bared. What a fright Randy had! He was ready to turn around and fly back home. But when he got as far as his favorite tree, the purple beech, he stopped there to rest and settle down. He was still shaking from fear.

By and by, when his nerves quieted down and things looked peaceful again, he started to grow bolder once more. He looked out over the tops of the trees in the direction of his home and decided he'd stick to his original plan to go exploring beyond the town. He had had his breakfast now and could fly high, out of harms' way.

He flew over the woods and the houses of the town until he came to unexplored territory. Beyond the town, there were farms with fields of wheat and corn. And beyond that, he flew over a river. How thrilling it was to see everything new! The earth was so big and wonderful. He flew and flew and flew. He flew over hills and valleys, over meadows and brooks, and he wasn't even hungry. He was so happy that he didn't want to stop at all.

Finally, he noticed that the sun was setting. How beautiful everything looked! He thought of what his mother had said about his favorite tree at sunset. "She's right," he thought, "everything looks more beautiful in the setting sun." Then he remembered that he was a long way from home, and that he'd better turn around if he wanted to get home before dark. He hated to do it; this was the best time of his life. He thought of how much fun it would be to tell his brothers and sisters about all that he had seen. He guessed that even his mother hadn't flown as far as he did that day. With this pleasant thought, he turned around and headed for home. It wasn't very long before he realized that he had flown all day without ever paying much attention to the direction in which he was flying. So now, he wasn't exactly sure of which way to turn to go back. This gave him a fright, but he quickly recovered and decided to try to look for landmarks: things that he had seen and that had impressed him on his way.

Randy quickly discovered, however, that one field of corn looked pretty much like another, and so did the hills and valleys. He flew faster and faster hoping to find something that he could recognize.

After the sun went down, night came on more quickly than he expected. At first, even though it was getting dark, he was determined to keep flying, but he finally realized that it didn't make much sense to fly when he couldn't see where he was going. He then found a tall tree and settled down for the night. It was the first time he had slept away from home, and it was very frightening. He heard all kinds of weird sounds

that made him tremble. The memory of that orange cat who had attacked him came back and frightened him all the more. What a night that was! He imagined cats to be hiding behind every tree, peering out at him. Once he heard an animal howling in the distance, and it made him jump so that he almost lost his balance.

"What could it be," he wondered? "Does it like to eat little birds?"

Not long after, he was startled by something moving in the grass beneath the tree he was in. He held his breath until he grew dizzy. Oh how he wished that he were home again with his mother and father and brothers. Why, oh why, hadn't he listened to them?

He finally fell asleep, but all of his dreams were of terrible cats who leapt out at him. Cats of every size and color. How terrible nightmares can be!

In the morning he woke up feeling a little better. The sun rose clear and it looked like it would be another beautiful day. He felt certain he would find his way home today.

He flew off deciding to skip breakfast. Everything he saw reminded him of what he had seen the day before. And the longer he flew, the more discouraged he became because he couldn't be certain that he had, in fact, actually seen that particular house or that particular barn or that particular hill before. Finally, the sun began to set again, and he grew ever so frightened and worried. He had only stopped to eat once that day, but although he had flown many miles, he wasn't certain whether he was nearer or

farther from home than when he had set out. When darkness came, he again looked for the tallest tree and settled there for the night. What a long time it took him to fall asleep! The night noises he had never noticed before were so loud and frightening. Once he heard the screech of an owl who was somewhere very near. This made him freeze with fear. He began to wonder if he would ever see his mother and father and sisters and brothers again. That night Randy cried himself to sleep.

The next morning he woke up feeling very hungry. He wasn't particular about what he ate and he didn't enjoy his food very much either. All he wanted was to get home, but he didn't know in which direction to fly. He would look one way, then another, but nothing looked familiar. Finally, he thought he saw a woods in the distance. He was very excited. He felt certain those would be his woods, and that he would get home again soon.

When he got there, however, he found that the trees belonged to a city park. How disappointed he was! How discouraged! At that point Randy Robin flew down on the head of a statue and began to cry.

"What will I do," he sobbed, "I will never see my home and family again." Just then he heard a voice.

"What's the matter, little robin?"

Randy turned and saw a pigeon.

"Are you lost?" asked the pigeon.

"Yes," answered the little robin. "I've been flying for two days, and I haven't any idea where I am."

Although he was embarrassed to cry, he couldn't help himself.

"What am I to do?"

"Do you know from which direction you came?" asked the pigeon.

"No," answered Randy Robin. "How stupid I was to leave home, and now I'll never find it again."

"Well, I admit it wasn't very bright to fly so far without knowing where you were going," said the pigeon, "but maybe I can help you find your way home again."

"How can you do that," said Randy, "when I don't even know myself where I've come from."

"They don't call me a homing pigeon for nothing," said the bird. "Now just tell me about your home. Do you live in the city or in the country?"

"We live in a woods at the edge of town," answered the robin, "but I don't even know the name of the town."

"What kind of trees grow in your woods?" asked the pigeon.

"We live in an oak," answered Randy, "and there are hemlock trees around us."

"Oh, there are oak and hemlock trees everywhere," said the pigeon.

"There are a lot of pine trees too," said the little robin.

"That's no help," said the pigeon, "there are pine trees all over."

"There are a few birches," continued Randy not too hopefully.

"Well, that tells us something," said the homing pigeon, "but not much. That could cover the whole northern part of the country, and that's thousands of miles."

The little robin put his head down with a sigh. "It's no use," he said shaking his head sadly. "It's hopeless. I can't think of anything that could even give you a clue."

The little robin tried to hold back the tears but that was hopeless too.

"Well," said the pigeon, "I'll say it's hopeless with an attitude like that! Com'on now. The most important thing is not to give up even when you are discouraged. Besides, no one ever accomplished anything with a dejected spirit. You've got to hope, and with hope comes courage. Now you just tax your brain a little more. Think of something near your home that you like."

Randy thought and thought. Finally he began to perk up. "There is one tree," he said, "that stands out among all the others. It is the biggest and the most beautiful in all the woods. And it's purple. It's a purple beech. My mother said that in the fall it becomes a deep purple and can be seen from miles around."

"Hmm," said the pigeon, "I think I know the one you mean. It's one of the biggest purple beeches I've ever seen. That's about 30 miles northeast of here."

"Really!" said the little robin, "do you really think you know the one I mean?"

"I wouldn't doubt it," said the homing pigeon. "Many's the time I've circled that purple giant and admired the greatness of it. Let's not lose time now. Do you feel strong enough for the journey?"

"Oh yes," beamed Randy, "I feel much better now. Can we start at once?"

"Sure thing," said the pigeon. "If we make good time we ought to be there before night fall."

"Oh, do you think so? I would be so very happy," said the little robin.

They took off into the air at once. They flew over the hills and over the valleys, over rivers and streams and farms and towns; the homing pigeon always leading the way. Although Randy didn't recognize anything that he had seen on the way out, he wasn't afraid anymore. In fact, he began to enjoy the scenery again, looking at the cows and horses, and the farmers plowing the fields. He began to dive down to get a better look at the little chickens that were in the farm yards. The homing pigeon called to him. "We're losing time. Don't forget that we want to make it home before night fall. There are only so many hours of daylight."

After this, Randy paid strict attention and tried to keep up with the homing pigeon. They stopped only once to eat in a farm yard where there were some red and white chickens. This was fun for the little robin because he had never been so close to these big birds before. What surprised him was the fact that they didn't seem to know how to fly. There were two pink little pigs in the yard, too, who gruntled constantly and dug up the ground with their snouts. How funny they looked!

They didn't stay there more than five minutes; however, and the little robin spent most of this time looking at the animals instead of looking for food.

They flew high over the steeple of a church and the little robin could see for miles. The sky was clear again today, which was another lucky thing. It's much harder to fly in bad weather.

Pretty soon the sun began to set.

"Do you really think we'll make it home before it gets dark?" shouted the little robin to the homing pigeon who was quite a bit ahead of him.

"We've just a few more miles to go before we will be able to see the big purple beech."

"Oh great," said Randy, and this made him fly a lot faster.

Sure enough, about a half hour later, the great purple beech came into sight.

"That's it! That's it!" shouted the little robin breathlessly. He was so excited he almost stopped in mid-flight. The homing pigeon was not as elated as the robin. "We're not close enough to be sure. Don't get your hopes up falsely," he warned. A few more minutes, however, and they were close enough to see and be certain that it was the right tree. Randy was so excited that he took off ahead of the pigeon and led the way.

One of Randy's brothers was the first to see him and shouted to the others. You have never heard such an uproar among robins before. The mother and father robin flew out to meet them and led them back to the spot, underneath a large blue spruce, where the other little robins waited.

What a feast they had! They offered the pigeon a big juicy worm to show how grateful they were to him for having brought back the little robin safely. He declined politely; however, saying that he preferred to eat seeds.

What a wonderful feast they had! And how happy they all were. The mother and father robin talked with the pigeon while the little robins chatted away. Randy told them all about his experiences while his brothers and sisters asked him questions about what he had seen and done. In fact, they stayed up way past their bed time, talking and laughing late into the night. The homing pigeon accepted their invitation to stay this night, but although they wanted him to stay longer, he told them that he had to return to his coop to attend to some business there the next day. He promised to come back and visit them as soon as he could. Finally, when they couldn't keep their eyes open any longer, the five little robins and their mother and father, together with the homing pigeon, went to sleep in the branches of the blue spruce. The little robin felt so safe and so happy that he had very pleasant dreams all through the night.